The
Donkey
Planet

The Donkey Planet

by Scott Corbett
illustrated by
Troy Howell

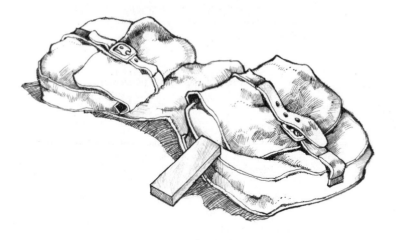

A Unicorn Book

E. P. Dutton   New York

Library of Congress Cataloging in Publication Data

Corbett, Scott.   The donkey planet.
(A Unicorn book)

SUMMARY: Two young scientists in disguise carry out
a dangerous mission on another planet.
[1. Science fiction. 2. Donkeys—Fiction]
I. Howell, Troy. II. Title.
PZ7.C79938Dp 1979 [Fic] 78-11455 ISBN 0-525-28825-2

Published in the United States by E. P. Dutton, a Division
of Sequoia-Elsevier Publishing Company, Inc., New York

Published simultaneously in Canada by Clarke,
Irwin & Company Limited, Toronto and Vancouver

Editor: Emilie McLeod   Designer: Patricia Lowy
Printed in the U.S.A.   First Edition
10 9 8 7 6 5 4 3 2 1

to Peg Deignan
my favorite librarian

1

The two youngest scientists at Space Center were Jason Scully and Frank Barnes. They worked on ordinary things like space shuttles and space stations, and dreamed of advancement to bigger and wilder projects.

Until he sent for them one day, neither had even met the center's top scientist, a man whose name sounded like X. He spelled it *Eks*. His work was so secret that only his closest associates knew anything about it, and they weren't talking.

"Eks wants to see you," said the director, not quite succeeding in masking his curiosity, concern, and—yes, perhaps envy. Jason had a reputation for being imaginative and resourceful. Frank was a sharp observer with a practical outlook, and had shown himself to be coolheaded and quick. Both had first-class scientific minds and both had shown promise in their work. But even so, what could Eks want with them?

Eks was a big man with black hair and a black mustache and a black patch over one eye. He looked more like a pirate than a scientist. Some of the others at Space Center, especially those who were jealous of him, said he was a little crazy. There was no question about his determination to let nothing stand in the way of any goal he set. And no one denied he was a great scientist.

He closed his office door, told Jason and Frank to sit down, and came straight to the point.

"I need two new assistants, and I think you might do. I have a special project for you. If that pans out all right you'll be working with me from now on. Are you interested?"

Interested? Who in the whole of Space Center would not have been interested? The startled glance that passed between Jason and Frank was like an exchange of electrical shocks. The atmosphere seemed suddenly to tremble with two of electricity's closely related potentials—power and danger. Jason found his voice first.

"It sounds like the chance of a lifetime, sir."

Eks's good eye glinted with hard amusement.

"It may be just that," he said.

Frank went straight for the facts.

"What is the project, sir?"

"I want you to run an errand for me."

"An errand?" The words were a letdown. But Frank persisted.

"Where to?"

Eks waved his hand casually.

"Oh, to a planet named Vanaris. We call it the Donkey Planet. It's in another solar system, not far past Sirius."

Sirius! Maybe his enemies were right about Eks! Maybe he *was* a bit mad. Sirius, the Dog Star, is one of the stars nearest to Earth—but they well knew how "near" that was.

"But, sir, Sirius is almost nine light-years from Earth." Jason tried to keep his tone controlled and level. "Even if we could travel at the speed of light, which we can't, a round trip would take us over seventeen years."

"My family wouldn't want me to be gone that long," said Frank.

Eks chuckled.

"You're right, of course. The speed of light, at only 186,000 miles per second, would be a horse-and-buggy way to travel around this vast universe of ours. But tell me, lads—have you ever considered the speed of thought?"

The speed of thought? Now what was he talking about? Just how advanced was the work Eks was doing?

"We can close our eyes and imagine ourselves to be *anywhere*, and we can do it instantly," he said. "Suppose we learned to control that ability, and direct it to a target?

"Each of us is merely a pattern, you know, made up of atoms and molecules that are constantly being replaced by others. Suppose you could project a thought-pattern into space? Suppose that thought-pattern, on Vanaris, would instantly attract to it the atoms and molecules needed to reproduce you?"

"You mean you can do *that*, sir?"

"Yes. But now, let me explain your errand. All you will have to do is take a few small bars of aluminum to Vanaris and bring back some very small pieces of quundar."

"Of what, sir?"

"Quundar. The Vanarians have no aluminum. They want some to study and analyze. We, of course, have no quundar. We would like to study it."

"Er—quundar, sir?"

"Quundar. It's an extremely heavy metal, 380 times as heavy as our heaviest metal. A gold coin the size of a fifty-cent piece would weigh a little under an ounce. A coin that size made of quundar would weigh 28 pounds."

He paused, saw the astonishment and interest in their faces, and seemed satisfied.

"Now, then," he said, "let me tell you something about the Donkey Planet."

2

"We call it the Donkey Planet because animals extraordinarily similar to our own donkeys are the principal means of transportation there," said Eks. "The Vanarians use them to ride on and to pull their carts. They're strict, stern, conservative people, the Vanarians. Even though their scientists are quite advanced, the people cling to old-fashioned ways. They don't have any oil to run motors with, and wouldn't want to pollute their atmosphere with its fumes if they did. So you will need a boy and a donkey when you get to Vanaris. The quundar will be heavy; you will need a donkey to carry it."

"What about the boy?"

"He will ride the donkey. Don't worry, they will be provided. But you will have to be careful, because the Isolationists have gained great power there, and they are against having any contact with other planets—except, perhaps, on their own terms, which we might not care for.

"The leader of the Isolationists, and the most dangerous man on Vanaris, is the chief of police in the town you will visit. His name is Gru. You will pass his place of business on your way to a rendezvous with a group of their scientists, with whom we've secretly kept in touch. Gru is dreaded all over Vanaris, and his power is growing. Be sure you do nothing to call yourselves to his attention. If that should happen . . . Well, I won't pretend this mission is without its dangers, but I'm counting on you to keep your heads and take no unnecessary chances."

Eks's "errand" was beginning to sound less and less routine. Jason challenged him.

"Unless the Vanarians look like us and speak English, I don't see how—"

"They do not look exactly like us, but your disguises will be perfect," said Eks. "The Vanarians resemble us the most closely of any life form we have yet discovered on other planets, but even they are not quite the same. The boy, for example, will have a small bump on each side of his forehead. When Vanarian children reach the age of fourteen or thereabouts the bumps become a nice pair of horns."

"*Horns?*"

"Oh, nothing devilish, merely a small, neat pair of horns. Quite attractive, really."

"You mean, we'll have horns?"

"No, that will not be necessary. I repeat, your disguises will be most ingenious, as you will see when you get there. And through other changes we will project with your thought-pattern, the matter of speaking the languages will be taken care of. They will be speaking Vanarian, but it will sound like English to you. And your speech will sound like Vanarian to them."

Next Eks told them exactly where to go and what to do when they reached Vanaris.

"All this should not take you long. A few hours, no more. In fact, it should be a snap for a pair of bright young fellows like you," said Eks with breezy confidence. "Now come with me and I'll show you the Black Box. That's what I call our thought-projection room, but don't let it disturb you."

As they followed Eks into his laboratory they had hardly time for more than a glimpse of the jumble of equipment in the famous workshop. Eks took them swiftly to a far corner, opened a door, and led them into a small, dimly lighted room with dark gray walls, ceiling, and floor. It was empty except for two pairs of upright waist-high poles topped with shiny metal balls, and a pair of saddlebags lying on the floor. Eks picked up the saddlebags.

"The aluminum is in these bags."

He showed them seven small bars of the metal, each no larger than a chocolate bar.

"Only give them six of these. Bring one back with you, so that we can determine whether its structure is affected in any way by the trip."

He returned the bars to their places in the bags. His good eye swept like a searchlight over his new assistants, Jason tall and thin, Frank squat and powerfully built.

"Here, Frank, you take charge of these," he said, draping the bags over Frank's shoulders. "You see, they're not very heavy now, but they'll be heavier when the quundar is in them. That's why the donkey will be needed."

"What about the boy?" asked Jason. "Are you sure he can be trusted?"

"Absolutely. Now, one last instruction, and this is important. Do not eat anything while you are on Vanaris. Their food would not agree with you. If all goes well, you will only be there two or three hours, anyway, so you won't need food."

His eye glinted at them again in an odd way.

"Your disguises will seem strange to you, but you will quickly come to understand how well they will protect you. Take everything in stride. Let nothing upset you. Remember that your changed situation will be only temporary, only a matter of a few hours. Make the most of your errand as an experience of immense scientific value. Any further questions?"

"One, sir."

"Well, Jason?"

"I always like to know the worst, so as to be prepared for anything. Suppose for some reason we were unable to project ourselves back from Vanaris to the Black Box. What then?"

Eks did not hesitate. He answered bluntly.

"In that case you would continue to exist on Vanaris—for as long as you could manage to support life there. Back here on Earth, the Black Box would contain a couple of empty bodies. What we on Earth call dead bodies."

There was a moment of silence.

"Oh, but don't let's talk about such unlikely events," said Eks, breezy again. "As I said, this whole thing should be a snap for you lads. Are we ready to begin?"

There was no backing out now. They both knew that. Backing out would mean the end of their careers at Space Center. Besides, who would not risk his life for a chance to visit a strange planet? What better thing was there to do with life than that?

"I'm ready," said Frank.

"So am I," said Jason.

"Good! Now, then. Each of you stand between a pair of those conductors, gripping a ball top with each hand. I will be outside at the control panel. A thought-print of a circle of trees around a clearing will appear on the wall in front of you. Look at it carefully, then close your eyes and concentrate. Take your places, and good luck!"

Eks strode outside, shutting the door behind him. In pitch darkness Jason and Frank gripped the ball tops with palms that were suddenly sweaty.

"Do you really think it will work, Frank?"

"If it were anyone but Eks, I'd say no."

A bright picture flashed on the wall. They saw a circle of trees, but all the trees were red and shiny, shiny as jewels. It was like looking at a TV set with

the color tuned in wrong. The leaves were shiny, the branches were shiny, and the trunks were shiny.

Jason shut his eyes. As he did so he could sense that the thought-print had vanished from the wall and the room was black again. But the picture remained bright and clear in his mind.

He opened his eyes.

3

The thought-print was still there, but the color had faded to a lifeless gray. Now, however, it seemed to surround Jason. He realized he was *standing* in it.

"It worked! We're here!"

He was surprised to hear how shrill his voice sounded. He turned to look at Frank.

Standing beside him was a small gray donkey with a pair of saddlebags on his shoulders, but Frank was nowhere to be seen. Jason looked around wildly.

"Frank! Where are you?"

The donkey shied sideways and stared at him with its big brown eyes. "Jason! Is that you?"

"Well, of course it's me, but—"

Then Jason realized it was the donkey that had spoken.

"Frank! Is that *you*?"

The donkey looked down at himself, and reared back.

"What in—? Are those hoofs mine?"

When Frank spoke he made a sort of low braying sound in a voice that was hoarse and harsh. He said some things about Eks that were as harsh as his voice, and finished with, "*That's* what he meant when he said a boy and a donkey would be provided! I'm the donkey—and you're the boy!"

"I'm what?"

"Look at yourself."

Jason looked down.

For a moment each of them had to fight off hysteria. Each made himself remember what Eks had said—that their "disguises" would be only a temporary expedient, that if they followed instructions they would soon return to Earth and their own familiar bodies. "Take everything in stride. Let nothing upset you." Yes, indeed, that was easy to say in a laboratory nine light-years from Vanaris!

After a moment Frank's new harsh voice shook up Jason once again.

"What's more," he said, "I wish you could see the bumps on your head."

Jason's hands clutched convulsively at his temples.

"Good grief! They feel huge!"

"From the looks of them, you must be close to fourteen," grated Frank. "Stick around here for a few months and you'll be sprouting your horns."

"I must look awful!"

"Not here," Frank reminded him. "If Eks is right, you'd look funny without them. Anyway, what are a couple of bumps compared to being a donkey?"

Jason began to win his own fight. Panic subsided. To be a boy again for a few hours—what was so terrible about that, bumps and all, considering the other wonders of their situation?

"Well, Eks told us our disguises would be perfect, and I guess he's right. But listen, Frank, think about *where* we are! We're on Vanaris! We're on another planet, nine light-years from Earth! Isn't that worth being a donkey for a few hours? Think what an experience you'll have, finding out what it feels like to be an animal! You're a scientist, you have to be ready to try anything!"

"I don't know about that. This is going pretty far!"

Frank stamped around, wriggling his long ears,

swinging his tail around, thinking things over. He put his head down in an absentminded way and nearly nibbled the gray turf. Then he jerked his head up and glared at Jason.

"Did you see what I just did? I almost ate some grass!"

Jason knew he was going to have to humor his colleague a little.

"Well, what's wrong with that, Frank? You'd be surprised how natural it looked. Of course, Eks said not to eat anything, so you'd better not try it, but . . ."

Frank blew out a tremendous snort that faded into a grumpy, sighing sound.

"Well, whether we like it or not, we're stuck," he said grimly. "Remember what Eks told us? When we've got the quundar we're to come back to this exact same spot, close our eyes, and think Earth. We're programmed to return *with* the quundar."

He paused, then added a chilling observation.

"That means we won't be able to get back without it."

4

Frank's words hit home, right in the pit of Jason's stomach. What Frank had said was true. Quundar was their passport back to Earth. Either they got hold of it or they would be trapped on Vanaris in the form of a boy and a donkey. And creatures from other planets were not welcome here.

"If things go wrong, you may be better off than I, Frank. There's no telling what that Gru character might do to me."

"Yes, but who wants to be a donkey for the rest of his life? I'll say one thing for Eks—he knows how to make sure we'll do our best to bring back what he wants. So we might as well get started."

Jason nodded. He glanced to his left.

"The road should be over in that direction. Let's see, now. All we have to do is go straight ahead on that road till we come to some thick woods. . . ."

"Listen for someone to whistle three times. . . ."

"Drop off the aluminum. . . ."

"Pick up the quundar. . . ."

"And come straight back. The sooner we get going, the sooner we'll get back here and be out of this mess. But let's have a good look around before we leave, so we'll know this spot when we see it again."

Everything around them was dull gray in color. The trees had long needles like Earth's pine trees. These looked as metallic as actual steel needles; yet when Jason cautiously touched the point of one it was soft and the needle bent. Around the base of the trees grew mushrooms two feet tall that were as clear and shiny as dark-colored glass. They, too, looked gray. Nothing was red, nor were the trees as shiny as they had been in the thought-print.

"What happened to all the color, I wonder? Was that print inaccurate? I think I'll mark a couple of these trees so we'll know them again."

Jason reached for his pocketknife—but there was no knife, nor any pocket. He looked down and realized he was wearing a one-piece garment that buttoned down the front. The legs ended just below his knees.

"A fine thing! I suppose this is what boys wear on Vanaris. Buttons all the way, too. No zippers here."

"Eks said the Vanarians were old-fashioned."

"Well, I'm still going to mark some trees."

Jason opened a saddlebag, took out a bar of aluminum, and gouged big X's on the trunks of several trees. The metal bit into the bark, which looked glassy and hard but was soft. The aluminum made deep marks that looked dark gray.

"That ought to do it."

"And don't forget," said Frank, "we're to bring back one of those bars."

"Right." Jason unbuttoned the shirtfront of the garment and slipped a bar inside. The metal was cold against his skin. The garment was belted at the waist. Above the belt the loose folds concealed any small bulge the bar might have made. Jason patted it and was satisfied. Next, however, he gave Frank a worried look.

"Well, I'm supposed to ride you, so I'd better get

on. I've never been much of a rider, and I've certainly never been on a donkey before, so hold still."

He swung a leg over and sat on Frank's back.

"How does that feel, my four-footed friend?"

"Okay, but don't squirm around." Frank let out a noisy donkey sigh. "I'm as dedicated as the next scientist, but this is the limit!"

"Giddap!"

"Don't get funny," said Frank, and he began to trot through the strange gray woods toward the road.

When they reached the road they saw their first Vanarian.

5

The man was riding a donkey slightly larger than
Frank. He was still some distance away, coming
toward them in the dim gray light.

"Would you look at that?" said Frank. "He *does*
have horns!"

It was true they were small horns, but they were
nothing that could have been hidden under a hat.

"Quiet!" said Jason. "When they get here, let me
do the talking. Ordinary donkeys probably can't talk
here, any more than they can on Earth."

"I won't say anything unless the other donkey
says hello."

For Jason it was the worst moment yet. What if the language thing did not work? What if the man said something he could not understand? What would he do then?

"H-E-E-E-E-E-H-A-W-W!"

The Vanaris donkey brayed.

Frank rolled one big, startled brown eye back at Jason.

"Do you suppose that was meant for me?"

"Maybe so. You'd better bray back."

"What do I know about braying?"

"Maybe it comes naturally. Try!"

"Well . . ."

Frank took a deep breath.

"H-E-E-E-E-H-A-W-W! Hey, not bad, huh?"

He was quite pleased with himself.

"Yes, that's great, but it's only half the battle." Jason was still worried about the language problem. The old man approaching them had a severe face that went well with his horns.

"Whoa! . . . Here, you, boy, out early, ain't ye?"

Though the man's tone was far from pleasant, Jason was relieved to find he could understand him.

"Yes, sir!"

"Been up to some mischief, have ye?"

"No, sir!"

The old man's eyes were small and mean. Jason began to believe that Vanarians might resemble Earth people pretty closely after all. He had met this kind of man on Earth—a crabbed, suspicious busybody who hated everyone, and especially children. Back on Earth at that very moment some old sourball just like him was probably giving some boy a hard time.

"Well, if I catch you stepping out of line around here I'll have the police after ye!"

He looked as if he might say a good deal more, but at that moment his donkey interrupted the conversation. A female donkey, she had been looking at Frank with melting eyes. Now she stretched out her neck and nuzzled him, nose to nose.

"Stop that!" snarled the old man, and whacked her on the head with a switch. Frank, flabbergasted, had already shied away backwards. The man stared at him, and snapped at Jason, "That your father's donkey you're riding?"

"Yes, sir," said Jason, unable to think of anything else to say. He dreaded the next question he expected to hear—"Who's your father?" Instead he got a surprise.

"What model is it?"

Again Jason could not think of what to say. What

model? Of all the crazy questions! But then he took a chance.

"Oh, it's brand-new!"

The man nodded.

"Thought so. Mighty fine donkey for a youngster to be riding around on!"

"I don't get to ride him very often," said Jason. "Will you excuse me, sir? My father's expecting me home, and I'll get it good if I don't hurry."

Without waiting to be asked, Frank trotted off toward town.

6

When they had gone far enough to be well out of earshot Frank muttered words of encouragement.

"Stop shaking, Jason. You did all right."

"I'm not so sure. I didn't like the way he looked at me. Not a good beginning. Not a good beginning at all."

"Did you notice he said we were out early? Maybe that's why the light is so dim."

To prove Frank's point, something happened at that instant that was wonderful but frightened them half to death.

The planet's sun began to rise.

The tip of the sun, deep blood-red in color, came up over the horizon and quickly broadened to a monstrous size, larger than anything they had ever seen before. It looked at least five times the size of Earth's sun.

As it rose, everything in sight turned red. The trees were red and shiny now, like the ones in the thought-print. The road was a light, dusty red. Where the sun's rays reached the giant mushrooms under the trees they glowed with a rich orange color. Even Frank was no longer a gray donkey, but something nearer to pink.

When the sun had risen completely it was still as red as Earth's sun is at sunset, but not much brighter.

"Did you ever hope to see anything that big in your life?" asked Jason, when he could speak.

"No, but I don't think it's quite as big as it looks." Frank was struggling to think like a scientist. "My guess is that Vanaris is a lot closer to its sun than Earth is to ours."

"Vanaris must be smaller than Earth, too. The horizon looks more curved. And considering how fast the sun came up, Vanaris must be rotating faster. Being so close to a sun like that, you'd think we'd be getting fried. It must be an old star, and not nearly so hot as our sun."

"And if Vanaris is smaller than Earth, it must be a lot denser, because the force of gravity seems about the same here. Maybe that's why they have heavier metals than we do."

Jason nodded. Then he grinned, and was glad to find his sense of humor was still working. Here on Vanaris he might need it.

"Well, anyway, it looks like you've got what it takes on the Donkey Planet, Frank. That lady donkey back there thought you were pretty cute."

Donkey or not, Frank let out a very recognizable groan.

"Oh, boy! We've got problems enough without that! Let's get moving! The more traveling we do while it's still early and there aren't many people around—or lady donkeys—the better."

They were near the edge of the town now. They came to a corner where their road crossed a wide, straight street. Both sides were lined with square houses, all very much alike, and mostly two stories high. In front of them were hitching posts and watering troughs. A few Vanarians were in sight, riding on donkeys or driving small carts pulled by donkeys. In front of one watering trough a man was washing a donkey. Another man was carefully brushing a donkey's sleek sides. From time to time he would stand back to admire his work. The donkey's hide was pink velvet in the sunshine.

"No wonder Eks calls this the Donkey Planet," said Jason. "It looks as if it's run on donkey power."

"We donkeys must do most of the work here," agreed Frank.

"H-e-e-h-a-w!"

The braying of a donkey in the distance made Jason look back.

The man they had passed on the road was coming their way now, and he was switching his donkey across the nose, as though he were angry with her for braying.

Was it because he had not wanted Jason to notice he had turned around?

7

"Frank, that old man is coming back this way."

"Fast?"

"No, but he's coming. I told you I didn't like the way he looked at me. Maybe something about us made him suspicious. Let's go on, but not too fast. That might give him the wrong idea."

"Or the right one." Frank began to trot ahead.

Not far from the corner, once they had crossed the wide street, they came to a building that did nothing to make them feel better. It was set back from the road behind a high wall with a wide pair of gates in it. Beside the gates stood a sentry. Even on Earth he would have looked like a policeman, although his uniform would have seemed very old-fashioned there. His helmet had slots in it that fit around his horns. Over the gate was a large sign with strange symbols on it.

"Can you read that, Frank?"

"No, but I don't have to read it to know a police station when I see one. This must be where that Isolationist leader hangs out. Eks said we would pass his 'place of business.' "

"You mean Gru."

"Yes."

Once again their timing seemed determined to be bad. First they had met an old man it would have been better to avoid. Now, turning his large donkey toward the gates of the police station, a man in a black uniform came riding toward them. There was something about the dark, horned face of the rider that suggested terrible power dreadfully used. The sentry suddenly snapped to rigid attention, then leaped to pull open the gate.

The rider glanced at Jason, and Jason's skin crawled as if something unclean had raised a welt on it. The deep-set eyes flicked on past him, seemingly incurious, and seconds later the gates had closed behind donkey and rider.

"Speak of the devil," muttered Jason. "That had to be Gru."

"Yes. Maybe it's my sensitive animal nature, but he didn't make a good impression on me at all," said Frank, trotting a little faster. "Let's see as little of him as possible. We've got to stay out of trouble. I wonder if that old guy is still coming."

"I don't know, but I don't like to keep looking back. I wish you were equipped with a rear vision mirror, like a car."

"Wait a minute. Let me do the looking. I just realized something. My eyes are in the sides of my head, so I don't have to turn far to look."

Frank checked and reported.

"I can't see him now."

"Then he can't see us, either, so let's make some time. Eks said it would only be a couple of miles to the woods where we'll trade metals."

The road they were following led them away from the outskirts of the city back into the countryside. In the strange sky above them, thin clouds began to form and cover the huge sun. Houses and fields and distant hills all turned a dull dark red, gloomy and sinister. Jason began to feel a deep dislike and fear of the somber planet. Nothing about it looked friendly, including the few Vanarians who passed by on the road. Some were men on donkeys, and some were riding in donkey carts. The only women they saw were two small, fat women riding in a cart. Jason was so surprised by their appearance he could hardly keep his face straight.

"Did you see their horns, Frank? They're even proud of them! You could tell that from the way they were all shined up."

"Looked just like nail polish to me."

A moment later they passed what appeared to be a large corral. In front of it several donkeys were tied up at a long hitching post. Two men were standing in front of them.

"Now, this is our latest model, the finest-bred donkey we've ever produced," one man was saying. "One of these will run twenty-five miles on half a bundle of hay."

"How much will you give me for my old donkey?"

"How long have you had it?"

"Eight years—and I wouldn't trade it in now, except that I need a larger model."

Jason and Frank kept moving, but they had heard enough to know they were listening to a donkey salesman and a customer.

"How do you like that?" said Jason. "They treat donkeys the way we do cars!"

"I don't like it," said Frank. "I'll bet it's no fun being an old used donkey here."

"I hope you won't have to find out."

8

Frank took another long look at the donkeys they had just passed.

"Eks said they were 'extraordinarily similar' to our own donkeys. I can't see much difference myself."

"Neither can I, but I never saw many at home," said Jason. "You're the first donkey I've ever had anything to do with."

"Same here!"

The country was no longer flat and level, but the road still ran straight ahead over low, rolling hills. As Frank trotted down a slope, the clouds cleared

away and all the various shades of red that sur-
rounded Jason and Frank became brighter again. By
the time they reached the bottom of the slope the few
trees in sight were as shiny as jewels again, and the
fields were carpets of scarlet. The sheen and sparkle
of it all cheered them up.

Ahead of them a side road forked off to the right.
At the fork in the road a tall, dark-haired girl stood
beside a dainty little mule, adjusting baskets slung
from the mule's sides.

"Well, look at that!" muttered Jason. "They *do*
have girls here, after all. I was beginning to wonder.
Now what do I do? Should I say hello, or not? Either
way I could be doing the wrong thing according to
local custom."

"Play it by ear. See what she does."

The girl surprised Jason in more ways than one.
By any standards she was pretty. The bumps on her
temples were so small they hardly mattered—in fact,
they were sort of attractive. She was dressed as simply as he was, but she had the beginnings of a figure
that would have been as easy on the eyes back on
Earth as it was here on Vanaris. Her dark eyes
watched them come with a level expression that was
neither bold nor demure. At the last instant, as they

passed, Jason decided to take a chance. He wouldn't speak, but he would at least be friendly.

He smiled and nodded. The girl looked surprised, but said nothing. In the meantime, Frank was growing more nervous than Jason, because the girl's donkey was looking at him with a melting gaze he had seen before. All at once the little donkey pranced forward and gave him an amorous nip on the hindquarters.

"Hey!" Frank made a wild leap forward, then swung around to glare at the flirt.

"Hixie! Stop that!" cried the girl.

"What's the idea? What do you think you're doing?" babbled Jason, doing his best to cover up Frank's slip of the tongue.

"What's the matter with *you*?" the girl retorted angrily. "Why did your donkey get so excited? Any normal donkey would have liked that! And what was that funny noise he made? It sounded like—"

"It's a trick I taught him. I'm sorry, we didn't mean any harm. Excuse me!" said Jason, and he turned to ride hastily away.

"What do you mean, *we*?" the girl asked contemptuously. "You've got some very funny manners!" she called after them as they fled.

"A fine thing!" growled Jason. "Her donkey nips *my* donkey and I have to apologize! And now we've made another Vanarian suspicious of us. I guess you don't speak of yourself and your donkey as 'we' here."

"I guess not. I'm sorry I yelled, but you'd yell too if someone bit you on the—"

"The Last of the Great Lovers, that's you," sighed Jason. "Man, could you ever be a Don Juan around here, if you only had the time!"

Both of them felt confused and upset by the strange emotions they were experiencing. Frank confessed first.

"The worst of it is, I caught myself thinking Hixie was really pretty cute!"

"Well, for that matter, I've seen worse than that girl," said Jason. "She's just about my age, too."

"Your age *now*," Frank reminded him. "You're an older man. Listen, the sooner we get this job done and leave this planet, the better. Life could get very complicated here!"

All in all, they were both relieved to find that by now they were alone on the road. Not a single Vanarian was in sight anywhere. They reached the top of a hill, and when they looked ahead, down the far slope, they saw something that cheered them up even more.

"Look! There are the woods!"

But then Frank pricked up his long ears.

"Hey, what's that? Do I hear someone coming?"

They both turned to see.

Frank was right.

9

A man on a large donkey, riding fast, had come into sight on the ridge of the hill behind them. He wore the helmet and uniform of a policeman. He raised his hand and shouted something.

"Go, Frank!" said Jason.

Frank went downhill full tilt toward the place where the road disappeared into the thick woods. Seen from above, the trees were red and shiny, but the place where the road plunged into them was like a dark blue tunnel. Rushing into it was like diving into an undersea cavern where everything was blue and green, and where the same mushrooms that had glowed bright orange on the edge of the woods were a deep purple.

"Get off the road as soon as you can, Frank!"

"Don't worry!"

Frank picked his spot carefully. He swerved off into the blue green underbrush with as light steps as he possibly could, trying not to leave visible footprints. He trotted deep into the woods, then stopped and stood still. Jason glanced up. Overhead the leaves were so thick they shut out the sun, and every leaf acted as a color filter, changing warm colors to cool ones.

Holding their breath, they listened. Soon they could hear the sound of hoofbeats. Would the policeman be sharp enough to see where Frank had turned off? Jason knew that if the hoofbeats slowed and stopped, he and Frank were in big trouble.

"Faster!"

They heard the policeman snarl at his donkey, and heard the crack of his whip on the donkey's flank. The hoofbeats pounded past. Jason and Frank breathed again.

"Now what?" said Frank in a low voice.

"I don't know. We ought to return to the road and keep going till we hear a signal—but what if the policeman decides to turn around and come back? How can we—"

A low whistle came from somewhere close by. Once. Twice. Three times.

They stared around them. Neither could see a sign of anyone.

From a nearby thicket came the sound of a voice, little more than a whisper.

"Over here."

Frank moved warily in that direction. Leaves rustled and parted. A small, bent man stood in front of them, a man whose deformities made Jason catch his breath.

His frail body looked as if it had been almost wrenched apart. Pain had carved his face like a knife. His burning eyes took in the expression on Jason's face, and he nodded.

"So you are the Earthlings. Excellent. My name is Speranz. You will pardon my appearance," he said in a whispery voice. "I have recently been questioned by Commander Gru. But don't worry—at that time I knew very little of what I know now, and I didn't give away anything important. The fact that he finally released me is proof of that."

"Who is that Gru? Is he your dictator, or what?"

"Not yet—but he will be if he isn't stopped soon. His ambitions go far beyond Vanaris, however. Vanaris is merely a stepping-stone for him. He wants to be the master of other planets as well. Yours, for example," Speranz added in a matter-of-fact way that startled Jason. "He's a very dangerous man. Our monarch and many members of our parliament oppose him—even many of his own higher officers dislike him and his methods—but so far he's been too clever for all of them. I hope you have brought the promised metal. We think it can help us contrive a means of—er—fighting Gru's influence."

"The metal is here."

"Good. Let me have the bags, and I'll make the exchange. I have colleagues nearby, but it would be better for you not to see them. The fewer of us you can identify, the better, should anything go wrong. And you needn't worry about me. If they should come for me again, I shall be dead before they can touch me."

Jason felt a sudden surge of resentment.

"Why couldn't we have been sent directly to this spot, instead of to those other woods? Then all this trouble could have been avoided."

Speranz shook his head.

"That was the closest spot that could be adapted to the tricky problem of getting you here. I haven't time to explain, but you can ask your Earthling chief about it later."

"He's got plenty of explaining to do, if I ever see him again!"

Speranz took the saddlebags from Jason, and as he did so his eyes suddenly twinkled. He patted Frank on the shoulder.

"It's quite all right for you to speak if you like, because I know about your disguise," he said. "In fact, it was I who suggested it."

"Well! I'm not sure I feel like thanking you," said Frank, "but I'm glad to meet you anyway."

"Good. Wait here. I won't be long."

10

Speranz took the bags and limped away into the woods. While he was gone neither Jason nor Frank spoke, but their thoughts were similar. Was Eks's purpose in sending them to Vanaris more than it seemed? Did Eks take Commander Gru seriously as a threat to Earth, seriously enough to help Gru's enemies? How much did Eks really know about the situation here on Vanaris?

When Speranz returned, the saddlebags were obviously much heavier. He was struggling along so painfully that Jason jumped off Frank to help. Together they lifted the bags onto Frank's back.

"Thank you. I'm afraid I don't have my former strength, or my voice. I can no longer speak any louder than this, since I was entertained by Gru. Now then, go straight back to the place where you arrived. With luck, no one will bother you."

"But what about that policeman? What if he turns around and catches up with us on the way back?"

"We were prepared for anything of this nature that might happen. By now he has ridden out of the woods and seen a boy on a donkey ahead of him in the distance near the top of the next hill. He will keep going. And if he should return this way . . . well, he will not leave these woods again."

Speranz handed Jason a piece of parchment-like material.

"Study this map. It is the safest way for you to return. Stay on this road only until you reach the side road I have marked—"

"I know the one," said Jason, remembering the girl and her donkey.

"Take that road until you reach the last street—"

"The wide one."

"Yes. Then follow the path marked on the far side of it till you reach the point of your arrival on

Vanaris. Memorize it carefully, because you must not keep it."

"I should say not. . . . All right, I have it." Jason showed it to Frank, who also studied it carefully. Then he returned the map to Speranz.

"Good," said Speranz. "Now, one last thing. Do not eat anything, especially our mushrooms. The great golden ones, the ones that look purple here in the deep woods, are healthy food for us, but they would make you ill. As for the small black ones, which have special uses . . ."

The twisted man stepped back and threw his arms wide.

"This is what the black mushroom can do in the course of dragging the truth out of a reluctant witness," he declared. Then he dropped his arms and added words meant to be reassuring. "You would not suffer in this way, however. If a bit of the black mushroom were forced down your throat it would kill you almost instantly."

"I see. Well, I'd prefer that," admitted Jason. He glanced around at the forest floor. "I haven't seen any small black ones that I know of."

Speranz smiled bleakly.

"You may be sure they do not grow wild. Now,

go. The small pieces of quundar are well wrapped. No one would think you were carrying such things, and they are of no great value here on Vanaris anyway. Go, and may fortune be with you!"

Feeling as though there were eyes behind every tree, they picked their way past bushes and under vines to the road. Now they were looking down a blue green tunnel with fiery red light at the end of it.

They had the heavy metal, and with it they were programmed for escape. The road to safety stretched straight ahead—yet nothing could have been less inviting. Leaving the cool protection of their hiding place to expose themselves once more in that red landscape was the hardest thing they had done. There was, however, nothing else to do.

At first, no one was in sight anywhere. It was like being on a deserted planet. They wished they were, but knew they were not. They went up each low, rolling hill dreading the sight of Vanarians on the other side. When they began to encounter some, riding donkeys, riding in carts, or walking, it was all Jason could do to try to look unconcerned as they passed.

One by one the landmarks they had noticed went by without incident. Soon they were nearing the fork in the road where the frisky Hixie had given them trouble, and they knew they no longer had far to go. Jason's spirits rose.

"We're going to make it," he muttered to Frank.

His timing was bad. Because at that instant two men who had been hidden by a line of trees rode out onto the road in front of them. One wore the helmet and uniform of a policeman. The other was the first man they had met on Vanaris.

"That's him!" cried the old man. "That's the boy, officer!"

11

The policeman threw the loop of a rope around Frank's neck and yanked it tight while the old man gloated.

"There will be a reward, won't there? I'll get a reward?"

"Yes, yes, you'll get your reward, Snigg," snapped the policeman. "First we'll worry about taking this —this whatever-he-is—to the commander. Ride directly behind him. Let's go."

For a moment Jason was paralyzed. He could not even speak. Obviously any pretense of being an ordinary boy was useless. The policeman knew something—but how much?

The officer kicked his donkey's sides and their procession began to move, with Snigg falling into line close behind, and the policeman holding the rope in one hand behind his back.

With his neck outstretched in an effort to ease the brutal tightness of the knotted loop, Frank followed the policeman. Then—

"Hang on!"

Rushing forward, Frank gave the policeman's donkey a savage nip. The donkey reared up, braying in pain, while Frank braced his legs and yanked back. The policeman tumbled off backwards, and when Frank's hindquarters slammed against the nose of Snigg's donkey, Snigg went flying, too. Cutting around the policeman's donkey, Frank made for the open road.

Somehow Jason managed to stay on. He pulled the rope loose from Frank's neck and threw it aside. For an instant he was exhilarated, but then a glance back made his heart sink. The policeman was already on his feet. How could they possibly escape the larger, faster donkeys?

But the side road was not far ahead, and when they

reached it Frank swerved into it, slipping and sliding around a hairpin turn. The road curved off to the right. Alongside the road at the curve was a watering trough, with several donkeys tied up in front of it. Behind the trough was a hedge.

"When I stop, you jump off and hide!" said Frank.

He ran straight to the trough and skidded to a halt. He stopped so abruptly that Jason went flying over his head and over the hedge.

Jason hit the ground, rolled over, and lay still, first seeing stars and then seeing something much worse. Someone was coming along a path close beside where he lay. He looked up and gasped. It was the girl he had seen that morning at the fork in the road.

She looked at him in amazement, then heard the sound of pounding hoofs coming on the road and hurried around the side of the hedge. Hoofbeats scrabbled to a stop, and the rough voice of the policeman put an end to any hopes Jason might have had.

"A boy on a donkey! Which turn did he take, up ahead?"

Jason rolled over, keeping down, but determined to make a run for it.

"The left one," said the girl.

Other hoofbeats sounded and slowed.

"Which way?" yelled Snigg.

"Left!" said the policeman, and they clattered away in hot pursuit.

The girl walked back around the hedge. Jason, still poised for flight, stared up at her.

"Why did you do that?"

She gave him a scornful look.

"Because I don't like Gru's kind of policemen."

Jason beamed at her.

"Good. Then we're on the same side. Listen, can you hide me somewhere till I get my bearings and can decide what to do? Find a safe place and I'll explain everything."

She considered briefly.

"I'll take you to my family's stables. They're near here. No one else is home now, so you'll be safe for a while—though no one is safe these days!" she added bitterly.

"Let's go." Jason stood up and looked across the hedge. "Oh, and could you bring Frank with us?"

"Frank?"

"My donkey. We'll need him. You'll see."

12

Showing good sense, the girl did not ask questions, but simply went and got Frank. Even at such a moment Jason could not help grinning, for if ever he had seen an embarrassed donkey it was Frank. Hixie was standing beside him at the trough, nuzzling his neck, and there was nothing Frank could do but stand there and take it.

"That will do, Hixie," said the girl sternly, and led a grateful Frank away. Jason joined them on the path and they hurried to the stables without a word being spoken. The girl swung open a door of the rough, low building. Frank walked inside, Jason followed. She came in and shut the door behind her. Around them was a smell not unlike the smell of hay on Earth.

Jason decided that even on Vanaris introductions were in order. "My name is Jason."

"Jason? I never heard of such a name before." The girl studied him warily. "Mine is Zil."

"Zil?" Jason tried to imagine a girl with a name like that back on Earth. "Well, Zil, get ready for a shock."

"What do you mean? Are you a Universalist?"

"A what?"

"Don't joke," said Zil in a severe voice. "Everyone knows what Universalists are."

"I'm not joking. Please tell me."

"You know very well that a Universalist is someone who believes in having contact with other planets!"

The tone of her voice told them something important. It told them where her sympathies lay.

"So that's it, Zil. Well, then, I guess I'm one, or I wouldn't be here trying to help *your* Universalists," said Jason. "You believe they're right, don't you?"

"Yes, but—"

Jason unbuttoned the shirtfront of his clothes, took out the bar of aluminum, and handed it to her.

She stared wide-eyed at the small gray bar.

"What is this? It looks like metal, but it's too light."

"It's a metal called aluminum. It comes from the planet Earth."

"From Earth? But how did it get here?"

"We brought it."

Zil's legs finally gave way under her. She sat down abruptly on the edge of a straw-filled manger.

"You mean . . . you're an Earthling?"

"Yes."

"But you look like one of us."

"We're disguised. We look different back on Earth—both of us. Back on Earth we're both grown men."

"That's right," said Frank. Zil stared at him and her eyes glazed.

Jason waved his hand in front of Zil's face.

"You shouldn't have done that, Frank!" he said, as he snapped his fingers.

Zil blinked. Her eyes widened and there was fear in them, desperate fear.

"Don't be afraid of us, Zil," began Jason, but she stood up and almost spat at him.

"I'm not afraid of *you*! There's nothing you could do half as bad as what will happen to me if—if—"

"What do you mean?"

"We have strict laws about intruders from other planets. Anyone who helps one in any way will be executed—after being questioned by the police . . . by Gru. . . ."

Jason tried to calm her.

"That's not going to happen to you. We're going to get out of here right away and take our chances. Right, Frank?"

"Certainly. No sense in getting Zil killed too."

Zil stared at Frank, still trying to grasp the reality of a talking donkey. Then she shook her head.

"You won't be killed. No one would dare kill you. Intruders must be taken alive, so that *they* can be questioned."

"By Gru?"

"Yes." Suddenly Zil sobbed. "Oh, why did you have to come here?"

Jason picked up the bar of aluminum.

"We came to bring this—but the less you know, the better, in case . . . Well, anyway, we're ready to return to Earth, if only we can get to a spot not far from here."

He could see sudden hope spring into Zil's dark eyes.

"Where? Where is it?"

He described the route he had memorized.

"I know the path. Did you come that way?"

"No." Jason described the road they had first taken, and again she nodded.

"My grandfather lives on a farm out along that road."

"Well, that's nice—but all we need to do is get to that path I told you about, and we'd better start now."

"No, wait." Zil backed away from Jason. "It may not be safe for you to leave here yet. Maybe that policeman has raised an alarm. Let me go ride around first and see what I can find out."

Jason glanced at Frank, then nodded.

"You'll be safer doing that than staying here, so go ahead."

"I'll hurry."

She slipped outside.

13

They waited in silence until the tension became un-
bearable.

"Jason, what will we do if someone else comes
home?"

"I don't know. Appeal to their Universalist sympathies, I suppose."

"How do we know Zil won't go straight to the
police?"

"If she was going to do that, why wouldn't she
have given us away in the first place?"

"She didn't know then that we were Earthlings."
Frank shrugged his donkey shoulders. "Not that I

think she will, but it's possible. She was scared."

"Yes, but she hates Gru."

"Well, I just hope she hates him enough."

They heard footsteps that did not sound like Zil's. They braced themselves. The footsteps approached . . . plodded past . . . faded away. They breathed again.

"Do you suppose we can wait till it gets dark?"

"I hope so."

Footsteps again. Light footsteps. The door was tugged open. Zil hurried in, alone—but the look on her pale face frightened them. She blurted out her news.

"They know. There are rumors everywhere that intruders have come from another planet. Every road and path out of town is guarded. Gru has offered large rewards for any information about you. And he wants you alive."

Earth suddenly seemed far more than nine light-years away. Frank snuffled out a soft donkey sigh. Jason glanced at him wonderingly.

"Gru must know something. But how could he? Two of his men were after us. We got away from both. What could either of them have told him that made him suspect us?"

"Something did, and that's all that matters. So we've got to get out of here or Zil will be in terrible trouble."

She shook her head.

"You wouldn't get two streets from here before you'd be arrested. And once they have you, they will soon have me."

"Would we have a better chance after dark?"

"No. There still wouldn't be any chance of getting past the police."

Jason nodded, and blew out his breath. Now that the situation seemed totally hopeless, now that there was nothing left to lose, he suddenly felt almost lighthearted. When he spoke again, his voice was strangely chipper.

"Well, then, I guess it's time to start looking for other ways."

"There aren't any," said Zil.

"There are always other ways," said Jason, and he began pacing.

Frank watched him with interest. "If you have any good ideas, let's hear them."

"I just might be getting one," said Jason, and he paced some more. Zil started to speak, but Frank nuzzled her arm.

"Let him alone. He's a pretty good idea man."

Presently Jason stopped again. He stared hard at Zil.

"Zil, how would you like to get rid of Gru?"

She was startled, but her reply was prompt.

"I'd do anything to get rid of him! I'd die for that!"

"You may. We all may. But . . ."

"Tell me what to do!"

"Well . . . Would the guards let you pass if you wanted to ride out to your grandfather's farm?"

She considered the question, then nodded.

"I think so. They're only on the lookout for boys, or boys on donkeys."

"And nobody would take you for a boy," said Jason with a grin. "All right, then . . ."

14

Following a route Zil had laid out for him, Jason walked along a quiet side lane with a basket on his arm. The basket was Zil's idea. Any boy seen on the streets might be looked at suspiciously, but a boy carrying a basket full of slices of golden mushrooms would be so natural a sight that he might well be disregarded—unless he tried to leave the town. She had even told him the name of an aunt of hers who lived near his destination, in case anyone asked him where he was going.

Even so, his heart beat painfully every time he had to pass another person. Glancing at someone else was almost a sure way of calling that person's attention to him, so he resisted doing so. He did his best to look carefree, unconcerned—and just a bit stupid.

There were few people in the tangle of side lanes, but when Jason reached the wide street that bordered the town he ran into trouble.

On the far side of that street scowling policemen were posted not more than fifty feet apart. Jason felt their eyes on him, and knew he had another important decision to make. If he walked down the street without even giving them a curious glance, wouldn't that in itself seem suspicious? Wouldn't any normal boy gawk at a row of policemen stationed fifty feet apart, and wonder why they were there?

He turned his head and gawked at them—and instantly decided he had made a mistake. One of the policemen returned his look with narrowing eyes, and called to the next policeman down the line.

Something had to be done quickly. Jason tried something that might have worked on Earth. Stubbing his toe, he pitched forward and sprawled on the street. His basket went flying, with mushroom slices spewing out of it in all directions.

A sweet sound reached his ears—the sound of rough laughter.

Scrambling to his feet he picked up the basket and

ran around collecting slices of mushroom, wiping them off clumsily against his shirtfront before putting them back in the basket. And as he did he looked up every now and then to glare at the policemen, which only made them laugh more.

Jason had remembered that no one takes someone seriously when he is making a fool of himself. Still shooting angry looks over his shoulder at the policemen he scurried away down the street and around the corner. A moment later he had reached the gates of the police station.

Now, as he confronted the sentry, Jason became vigorously self-important.

"There's a big reward for information about a boy on a donkey, isn't there?" he asked in an excited voice.

The sentry looked down at him scornfully.

"That depends on which boy and which donkey. Now move along."

"I know which one, all right. He's from somewhere else!" cried Jason. "And I have important information about him for Commander Gru!"

The sentry's expression changed. He studied Jason uncertainly, but he still blustered.

"What do *you* know, boy? Just tell me, and *I'll* decide whether—"

"You'd better let me see Commander Gru *in person* or you'll be in trouble!" said Jason, stuffing his voice with all the arrogant confidence he could. He knew that menials who worked for monsters like Gru lived in constant dread of making a mistake. The sentry licked his lips, pulled open the gate, and called inside.

"Here's a boy who says he knows something," he bawled, taking Jason's basket away from him and shoving him roughly inside.

Standing in the courtyard outside the main building was an officer who did not look as thick-witted as the sentry.

"Well, what is it?" he asked. "You may tell me anything you know, and I'll decide whether or not to bring your information to the commander's attention."

Jason reached inside his shirtfront and brought out the bar of aluminum. Still speaking with the enormous confidence he wished he truly felt, he said, "The commander will want to see me personally when he sees what I've brought."

"What is that?"

He handed the bar to the officer, who examined it with growing astonishment.

"What *is* it, boy?"

"It is not a metal we have here on Vanaris, sir."

The officer stared at him, and at the metal.

"Wait here," he said, and hurried inside the building.

15

Gru sat behind a heavy, boxlike desk balancing the aluminum bar on the palm of his hand. His face was long and dark, and almost handsome in an evil, malignant way. His horns were black. Jason remembered the way his skin had crawled at the mere sight of Gru earlier that morning, and felt an icy sort of fear. Did Satan walk up and down on other planets besides Earth?

Commander Gru smiled, and his smile was more frightening than all the scowls of his policemen. He held up the bar.

"And what is this?"

"It is a metal called aluminum, sir."

"And you are the intruder."

"One of them, sir."

"One?"

"Yes, Commander. There were two of us in our spaceship, and we were so well disguised that I don't understand how you were clever enough to suspect us. At any rate, you have got the best of us, so now I've come to offer you a bargain—the greatest bargain any living being has ever been offered in the universe."

Gru placed the bar of aluminum carefully on the desk, then eyed Jason with cruel amusement.

"*You're* going to bargain with *me*?"

"Yes, sir. We have an expression on Earth—"

"*Earth?*" Gru started to his feet, staring. "You're from Earth?"

"Yes, Commander."

Gru continued to stare for a moment, then sat down again.

"Earth," he said in a soft voice.

"We say, if you can't lick 'em, join 'em. I want to join forces with you. If you will agree, I can make you not only the master of this planet, but of others as well."

Ambition blazed up in Gru's eyes, but he was not so easily persuaded.

"What are you talking about?"

"We came hoping to make contact with others here on Vanaris, but we failed. You have won."

"What others?"

"I don't know."

Commander Gru sighed, and took a small box from under his desk. He set it on the desk top, opened it, and took out a small black object.

"I don't want to hear answers such as, 'I don't know.' I want the truth, I want to hear everything you know. Do you have any idea what this is?"

Jason stared steadily at the thing in Gru's hand.

"It is the black mushroom, and it won't do you any good, because it will kill an Earthling. I said I don't know, and I meant it. My Earthling masters are clever, too. They saw to it I knew as little as possible about the most important aspects of our mission. It is my companion who is programmed with all the information you really need."

Gru's eyes widened, and he smiled again.

"The donkey! Now, that *is* clever!"

Jason was genuinely impressed by Gru's rapid deduction. And he was quick to flatter the commander's vanity.

"Amazing! Sir, how did you ever guess?"

He was right about Gru's vanity. The commander could not resist explaining.

"To hold the position I do, it is necessary for me to think more, to notice more, to understand more than ordinary Vanarians. First, an old busybody turned up this morning with a report of a boy on a donkey who didn't look right to him. He's always reporting people, so I thought little of it at the moment—until I remembered a boy on a donkey I had noticed passing only minutes before. I remembered that the boy had looked at me, which was natural—but that the donkey had also looked at me. In an interested way, that is, with an obviously intelligent interest no ordinary donkey would have displayed."

"That was us, sir."

"Of course. I sent a policeman after you. The fool has not yet returned. I also had another policeman waiting for you to come back, however—"

"He almost got us."

"He was a fool, too. But he did report one interesting detail. He said it sounded as if the donkey spoke to you, as if it said, 'Hang on!' "

"It did."

"By the time I had his report I knew I could take

no chances. So! A talking donkey. That alone will be worth seeing. Where is this donkey, and your spaceship?"

"I will lead you to them, Commander, but I suggest that unless you wish to share your power with others, we go alone. I don't know the details, but I do know that the donkey is programmed to recite a great deal of technological data. It may be important to know how much of it you will want to make public, and how much you will want to control for your own advantage."

Gru's eyes narrowed, and then he sat back and rolled out a deep, scornful laugh.

"What kind of fool do you think I am? Do you think I would go alone with you into an ambush, so that your confederates could kill me and you could escape?"

"I have no confederates except the donkey, and it could hardly kill you. Very well, I'll draw you a map showing exactly where the donkey and the spaceship can be found," said Jason. "Send out your men to surround the empty spaceship and bring the donkey back here—and you'll never learn a thing."

Gru had stopped laughing. He picked up the

black mushroom, twirled it slowly between his fingers, and put it aside.

"Won't I? We have other resources besides this."

"The donkey cannot give up its secrets unless I order it to repeat them—and do so of my own free will. If, to avoid being tortured, I agreed to give the order *not* of my own free will, the donkey's sensors would detect the difference and the donkey would not speak."

Jason leaned forward and continued with all the bitterness he could muster. Thinking about Eks helped.

"Commander, our chief Earthling scientist deliberately sent me into an impossible situation here on Vanaris. After this failure it would not be safe for me to return to Earth—alone. So nothing would suit me better than to make him pay for this dearly. If you have any ambitions concerning the planet Earth, who could be more helpful to you than an Earthling? Of course, I don't blame you for not trusting me, so let me make one more suggestion. I will draw the map showing the place we will visit. Have your men surround the area, but stay far enough from the center so that they will not be able to see or hear anything."

He pointed to the bar of aluminum.

"And please bring that, sir. We will need it."

Gru's dangerous eyes studied Jason for a long time. Then he rose and went to the door.

16

Mounted on a small donkey, Jason rode out of the police station courtyard alongside the large donkey ridden by Commander Gru. At the crossroads ahead of them a squad of policemen watched them approach with ill-concealed excitement.

The officer Jason had spoken with in the courtyard stepped forward.

"Are the men posted as I ordered?" asked Gru.

"Yes, Commander. How many of us do you wish to accompany you?"

"None."

"None, sir?" The officer was astounded. He had

the courage to show his disapproval. "But, sir, is that wise? If anything should go wrong—"

"I assume sole responsibility for the prisoner!" thundered Gru. "Get out of my way."

Stony-faced, the officer stepped back, and they rode on. Now they were on the road Jason and Frank had first traveled that morning. Jason thought of the startling sunrise, and of their unlucky meeting with Snigg. He watched intently for the place where they would turn off into the woods.

"Here, Commander," he said finally, and Gru nodded.

"So far, your map was accurate."

They rode in through a scattering of trees, and with every step his donkey took, Jason's heart seemed to pound harder. The circle of trees was very close now. Any moment Frank should come into sight. . . .

"What are those marks on the trees?" asked Gru, pointing ahead. "Is that the place you described?"

Jason stared ahead and his carefully worked out plan crumbled to bits in his mind. Frank was not there—Frank and the Vanarian metal that was their sole passport back to Earth. Had Zil been stopped? Had she been unable to ride Frank past the police lines?

"And where is our wonderful talking donkey?" Gru continued in a silky voice. "I hope for your sake—"

Underbrush trembled nearby. It rustled, and parted. A donkey's head protruded itself solemnly into the open.

"I thought I'd better stay out of sight until you came," said Frank.

Jason discovered he still had lungs, and began using them again. Gru caught his own breath at the sound of the donkey's voice, and when he spoke his voice trembled with excitement.

"So it is true. It is really true." But then cold anger darkened his face. "I will want to know who brought the donkey here. No donkey wanders riderless on Vanaris."

"Yes, Commander." Dismounting, Jason held up his hand. "If I may have the aluminum bar I will position it on the donkey and give the necessary order."

Almost ceremoniously, and with great condescension, Gru handed him the bar. Hoping his legs would support him, and not look as shaky as they were, Jason walked over beside Frank. He placed the bar between Frank's long ears and held it there.

"I order you to repeat the data."

Frank faced Gru, looking up into his face, and spoke slowly and very clearly.

"In a very short time, Commander, you will have an interesting problem to work out. Now, Jason—think Earth!"

The last thing Jason saw was Gru pulling out some sort of weapon.

17

When he opened his eyes Jason was still on his feet, but Frank was flat on the floor beside him— the regular two-legged Frank, securely pinned down by the saddlebags.

"Take these bags off my neck!"

Jason found he was still holding the aluminum bar. He thrust it into his pocket—he had pockets again—and took hold of the saddlebags. It was all he could do to lift them aside.

"Gru is finished!" crowed Jason. "If he goes back and tells the truth, they'll say he's gone crazy. But no matter what story he tells, he can't produce the prisoner!"

Then, as Frank stood up, Jason grabbed his arm. "But what about Zil?"

"Don't worry. She's safe and sound at her grandpa's farm."

The door of the Black Box opened. Eks looked in at them with a bright gleam in his good eye.

"Ah! It's you, is it?"

"Who did you expect?" snapped Jason. "Here's your quundar."

Eks took the bags and hoisted them up and down with one powerful hand.

"Feels good. Must be quundar in here, all right. Congratulations! From now on you'll be working with me. Now, come and tell me exactly what happened."

Jason glared at Eks, then exchanged a glance with Frank. The steely glint in their eyes agreed.

Jason patted away a yawn, and shrugged.

"There's nothing much to tell," he said.

"That's right," said Frank. "It was a snap, just as you said it would be. A jackass could have done it."